This book belongs to:

Evan,

Cherish Wildlife!

9/4/11

A Busy Spring for Grandella

the
Gray Fox

Story and Photography by

Margie K. Carroll

Margie Carroll Press
Holly Springs, Georgia

Special thanks to Esther, Doris, Carol and Linda.

Margie Carroll Press
P.O. Box 581
Holly Springs, GA 30142

for Sandy

Hello Friend!

I must tell you about the busy spring I had. My name is Grandella and I was born under the breezeway of this old log cabin.

Dad and Mom cared for my two brothers, Albert and T.J., and me in the cool dark den.

For several weeks we snuggled next to Mom and listened for Dad to bring her food.

This is all we could see . . .

Nothing!

Finally, Mom said we were old enough to go out and play!

I smelled fresh air.

I saw a barn on the hill.

Playing outside was fun most of the time!

"Ouch, Albert! Stop that," I complained.

My brothers, T.J. and Albert, liked to scare each other.

While I was exploring I found a snack. But grass didn't taste good. Luckily, Mom came over and let us nurse.

"Mom, when may we go to the barn on the hill?"

Mom whispered, "When you grow up, Grandella."

So, I contented myself by watching my brothers.

Albert spied on T.J.

He ate grass, too!

One day someone was watching me.

Yikes!

Dad was a very good hunter.
He brought us voles, mice and rats.

I was good at peeking.

Very good.

Sometimes I could not see my folks.

But they were always watching us.

Dad and Mom taught us how to be smart foxes.

They showed us how to be alert and look . . .

smell . . .

and listen for danger.

We learned how to walk silently. We were becoming sly foxes.

Albert and I watched and learned from Mom and Dad.

T.J. listened sometimes, but mostly he stayed busy doing other things.

T.J. prowled with Albert.

We hunted and proudly showed our catch.

We adored our Mom.

I was growing up.

"Mom, am I big enough to go to the barn on the hill?"

"No, Grandella, you must sleep and eat more before you are ready," she replied.

So, we napped and rested.

We slept in the afternoon sun. Even Mr. Groundhog joined us.

Sometimes I couldn't nap. All I could think about was the barn on the hill.

Besides resting, we ate a lot!
Dad brought us great surprises.

Mom was bathing me one morning when she whispered in my ear, "Grandella, I am so proud of you and your brothers. Tomorrow I have a big surprise for you."

You guessed it! We got to go play in the barn on the hill.

That was my busy spring. I hope you had a busy spring, too.

Your friend,

Grandella

Fox Facts

The Common Gray Fox is a member of the dog family and, surprisingly, it is a good tree climber and often hides in trees. This canid has well-developed teeth, strong nonretractable claws and acute senses of smell, sight and hearing.

Gray foxes are omnivorous, eating small mammals, insects, fruits, birds, eggs and plant material, including corn, apples, persimmons, nuts, cherries, grapes, grass and blackberries. In late summer grasshoppers and crickets are often a very important part of the diet. They are timid, elusive and primarily nocturnal.

Range: Most of the U.S., but not in the Rockies or parts of the Great Plains. Age expectancy: Gray foxes can live six to ten years in the wild.

Gray foxes mate for life and form a range together. The female gives birth to 3-10 all black young, called kits, in an underground den which was dug by another creature. The male will not den with the female and their young, but he is always somewhere close by.

Oftentimes one of the parents will do the hunting while the other stays near the den to protect their young from any potential danger. However, both parents share the duties of hunting and caring for their young.

Resource Vocabulary

- adaptation: the process of adapting to something (such as environmental conditions)
- agile: moving quickly and lightly
- breezeway: a roofed, open-sided passageway connecting two structures, such as a house and a garage
- canid: any of various widely distributed carnivorous mammals of the family Canidae, which includes the foxes, wolves, dogs, jackals and coyotes
- den: the home of a wild animal; lair
- fur: the thick coat of soft hair covering the skin of a mammal, such as a fox or beaver
- habitat: a place where an animal naturally lives or a plant naturally grows
- kit: a young, often undersized fur-bearing animal
- mammal: a warm-blooded animal, such as a human being, dog or whale, the female of which produces milk to feed her babies
- monogamous: having one mate
- nocturnal: most active at night. Many animals, such as owls, foxes and bats, are nocturnal.
- nurture: to promote or encourage the development of
- omnivorous: feeding on both animal and vegetable substances
- offspring: a child or animal as related to its parent
- prey: an animal hunted or caught for food
- shelter: something that provides cover or protection, as from the weather
- vegetation: the plants of an area or a region; plant life
- vole: a small rodent with a stocky body and a short tail
- warm blooded: animals that keep their body temperature at a constant level
- woodlands: land having a cover of trees and shrubs

Questions for Young Readers

Where was Grandella (and her brothers) born?   under a breezeway

What did Grandella see when she first stepped outside?   the barn on the hill

Albert and T. J. loved to scare each other.   T or F   true

Who fed the fox kits?   mom and dad

What did the fox kits eat?   mice, rats, voles and milk

The mother went hunting with the father.   T or F   false, She stayed with the fox kits.

Before Grandella could go to the barn on the hill, she had to: Grow up

What animal was watching Grandella?   a cat

What did Mr. Groundhog do in the afternoon sun?   sleep

What was Grandella's surprise at the end of the story?   She got to go to the barn.

The images used in this book were taken "In the Valley" at the Corra Harris homeplace out of Pine Log, Georgia. The owner, Mr. Jodie Hill, kindly gave me a key to the unoccupied place and allowed me to photograph the wild foxes and buildings. In 2009 Mr. Hill gave the Corra Harris Estate to Kennesaw State University in Kennesaw, Georgia.

Margie K. Carroll lives in Canton, Georgia, where she enjoys the company of deer, raccoons, rabbits, numerous song birds and several alert cats at her studio in the woods.